Room *for* a Stepdaddy

Jean Thor Cook

Illustrated by

Martine Gourbault

ALBERT WHITMAN & COMPANY
MORTON GROVE, ILLINOIS

Joey wished Daddy still lived at home, that he would come through the door, swing Mommy around in a circle, and plant a big kiss on her cheek.

That didn't happen anymore.

There was a stepdaddy at Joey's house. His name was Bill.

Bill gave Joey warm mittens to build snowmen, tucked surprises in his pockets, and bought Joey a sled to slide down hills.

But gifts were not what Joey wanted. They only made him more lonesome for Daddy.

One day Bill sat on the couch with Joey. "Come close to me, and I'll read you a story," he said.

"Not now," Joey replied, moving away.

Joey didn't want to be near anyone but Mommy and Daddy.

Later, Mommy said, "Joey, I know you're still sad that Daddy has left and Bill is here."

"Yes," answered Joey, with a sniff.

"I'm sorry," said Mommy, cuddling him on her lap. "I think you'll feel better in a little while."

The next week, Daddy invited Joey to stay at his cabin. They tramped in the snowy woods and skated on the lake.

After the weekend, Daddy brought Joey home. He tucked him in bed and then stayed to visit with Mommy and Bill. They told each other they'd all try to do what was best for Joey.

Joey heard them talking. He pulled the covers over his head. "Don't forget me, Daddy," he whispered.

When winter snows had melted and tulips flashed bright colors, Bill surprised Joey with a puppy. Joey named him Patches because he was white with brown spots. Joey liked Patches's floppy ears and friendly tongue.

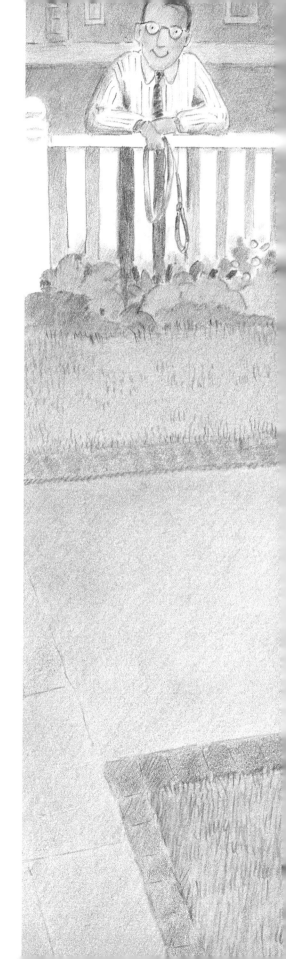

"Bill, I can't find Patches!" called Joey one morning. "He chased a cat and didn't come back!"

Tears splashed down Joey's cheeks.

Bill took Joey's hand, and together they searched. They found Patches in front of the cat's house, looking up and down the street.

"He was watching for me," said Joey.

"Yes, he knew you'd find him," said Bill.

Patches wagged his tail and jumped to lick Joey's face.

"Now let's go home," Joey said to Bill and Patches.

During spring, Joey and Daddy went back to the cabin. Daddy took Joey to hear frogs croak in a pond. He scooped up a squirmy frog for Joey to touch. Joey petted the frog before it jumped down and hopped away.

C an we go to the park to play ball?" asked Joey when summer brought hot days.

"Only if we buy ice-cream cones!" teased Bill with a big grin.

Together they tossed a ball high in the air, back and forth,

until Joey was tired.

"I'm ready for ice cream!" said Joey.

They walked home licking cones, Bill's hand on Joey's shoulder.

Daddy said summer was for playing in the water. He taught Joey to swim and caught him when he jumped off the dock. He told Joey that love was like the sand on the beach. There was so much to share that Joey would always have enough to go around. He could love them all: Mommy, Daddy, and Bill.

Soon summer passed, and school began.

Bill walked Joey to kindergarten that first day.

"I'll be back," Bill promised. "You can be sure I'll be here when it's time to go home."

Joey listened to stories, painted a picture, and sang a song with the other children.

When the teacher said good-bye, Bill was there by the door with Patches, just like he'd said he'd be.

Bill gave Joey a hug and took him home to Mommy.

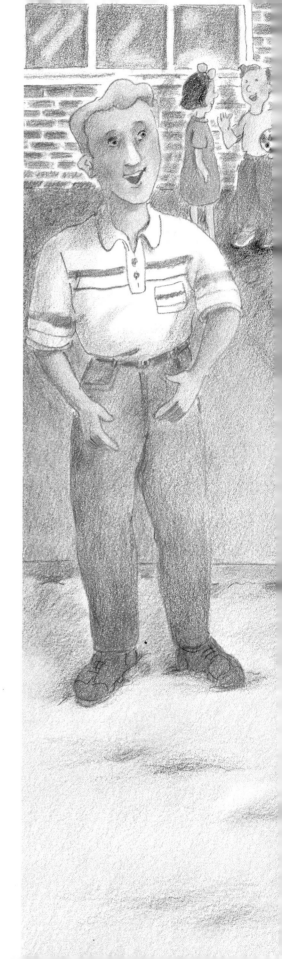

Daddy came to school, too. He stayed the whole morning. He pushed Joey on the swings and clapped when Joey turned somersaults on the bars.

Another day, Daddy brought everyone cupcakes for Joey's birthday.

On a fall afternoon, Bill raked leaves and Joey jumped into the piles.

When it got close to dinner, Bill said he had to finish the raking.

But Joey kept jumping. Then he threw the leaves into the wind, and they scattered back over the lawn.

Bill hollered, "Stop!"

Joey got angry. He stamped his foot and yelled, "I won't!
Only Daddy can make me!"

Bill gave Joey a time-out for five minutes.

Joey sat on the step a long while—too long, he thought.

"Bill, can I get up?" he finally asked.

Bill laughed. "Now *I'm* the one who's in trouble," he said.
"I forgot to notice when your time-out was done!"

Before fall ended, Daddy took Joey to the country again.

He showed him how squirrels carry nuts to their nests and how geese fly in a vee to go south.

Joey shivered in the cool air.

"Let's make cocoa," Daddy said.

Joey and Daddy raced each other to the cabin.

Joey wrapped three presents when the winter holidays came.

One for Mommy.

One for Daddy.

One for Bill.

Joey would give Daddy his gift tomorrow, on their special day.

"Come in!" he called to Mommy and Bill after all the ribbons were tied.

Joey held up the three presents for Mommy and Bill to see. He climbed on Bill's lap.

As the stars winked outside, Joey laid his head against Bill's shirt.

He thought about Daddy and how happy he would be to get his present.

Then Joey snuggled deep into Bill's arms.

It was warm and cozy there.

For all my grandchildren. J.T.C.
For my friend Marian. M.G.

Library of Congress Cataloging-in-Publication Data

Cook, Jean Thor, 1930-
Room for a stepdaddy / written by Jean Thor Cook ; illustrated by
Martine Gourbault.
p. cm.
Summary: Joey has trouble accepting his new stepfather, but the constant love of his father, mother,
and stepfather finally convinces him that there is love enough to go around for everybody.

ISBN 0-8075-7106-7
[1. Stepfathers—Fiction.] I. Gourbault, Martine, ill.
II. Title.
PZ7.C7698Ro 1995
[E]—dc20
95-3128
CIP
AC

The text typeface is Garamond.
The illustrations are colored pencil.
The design is by Karen A. Yops.